Qillak

Written by Ned Jensen
Illustrated by Mark Wilson

The arctic lands of northern North America are not good for farming. During the summer, the sun never sets and the days last for twenty-four hours. In the winter, there's no daylight and the nights last for twenty-four hours.

It's very cold, and there's not much soil on the land for growing plants. The people of these lands are Inuit. Long ago, they lived off the sea and hunted seals and walruses in boats called kayaks.

For two years, Qillak watched his older brother paddle out to sea. His brother would go and hunt with his father and the men of the village. Qillak dreamed of the day when he would hunt for seals. In a few months, he would be old enough. Qillak thought about that day, and he grew more excited as it got nearer the time.

Qillak had watched the men and older boys in his village build their kayaks since he was a little boy. He had watched them very carefully. Now the time had come for him to build his own kayak. Qillak knew what he had to do. It was a long, hard job.

First, Qillak had to build a wooden frame. Not many trees grow in the arctic lands, so Qillak walked along the seashore looking for driftwood. After four weeks of looking, he had collected enough wood to build the wooden frame. Qillak used tools made of sharp stones to shape the wood into the frame for his kayak.

Soon, Qillak was ready to tie the pieces of the frame together. He had collected and dried the guts of seals that men in the village had hunted. He used the dried guts to tie the pieces of wood together. Qillak's brother helped him by holding the pieces of wood together, and soon the kayak's wooden frame was finished.

Now, Qillak needed some sealskins to cover the wooden frame. He planned to trade some of the driftwood he had collected for sealskins. Qillak went to the seal hunters and in a few days he had enough sealskins to cover the kayak's wooden frame.

Qillak's mother had sewn the sealskins for his father's and his brother's kayaks. Qillak asked her if she would sew his sealskins, too. His mother was happy to help, and Qillak helped her by chewing the edges of the sealskins to make them easier to sew.

Before Qillak could go out to sea, he needed a strong, wooden paddle. He searched the seashore for a piece of driftwood big enough to make a paddle. Finally, Qillak found just the right piece of wood. He used his sharp tools to shape the driftwood into a paddle.

Qillak was very pleased with the kayak and the paddle he had made. He took them down to the sea, and his brother showed him how to paddle. Qillak paddled his kayak in the sea every day, and soon he was ready to go out hunting with the men and other boys.

Qillak's big day finally came when he had his birthday. Now he was old enough to go out with the others. For a long time Qillak didn't hunt, he just paddled along and watched how the men and boys used their harpoons.

At last, the day came when Qillak's father gave him his own harpoon, and they paddled out to sea. Qillak saw many seals, and many times he threw his harpoon but he missed them all.

As the day was coming to an end, Qillak saw a large seal. He paddled close to it and threw his harpoon. This time he didn't miss!

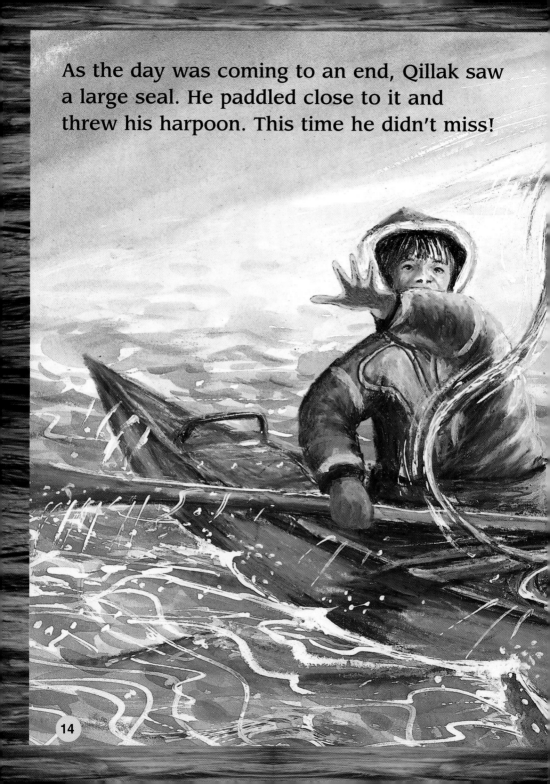

On his first real hunting trip, Qillak caught a seal. That night the village had a big party. Everyone was happy, Qillak had become a real hunter.